MW01267804

The Argument

Alexandra Gersten-Vassilaros

A Samuel French Acting Edition

SAMUEL
FRENCH

FOUNDED 1830

SAMUELFRENCH.COM
SAMUELFRENCH-LONDON.CO.UK

FOR PRODUCTION ENQUIRIES

UNITED STATES AND CANADA
Info@SamuelFrench.com
1-866-598-8449

UNITED KINGDOM AND EUROPE
Plays@SamuelFrench-London.co.uk
020-7255-4302

Each title is subject to availability from Samuel French, depending upon country of performance. Please be aware that *THE ARGUMENT* may not be licensed by Samuel French in your territory. Professional and amateur producers should contact the nearest Samuel French office or licensing partner to verify availability.

MUSIC USE NOTE

Licensees are solely responsible for obtaining formal written permission from copyright owners to use copyrighted music in the performance of this play and are strongly cautioned to do so. If no such permission is obtained by the licensee, then the licensee must use only original music that the licensee owns and controls. Licensees are solely responsible and liable for all music clearances and shall indemnify the copyright owners of the play(s) and their licensing agent, Samuel French, against any costs, expenses, losses and liabilities arising from the use of music by licensees. Please contact the appropriate music licensing authority in your territory for the rights to any incidental music.

IMPORTANT BILLING AND CREDIT REQUIREMENTS

If you have obtained performance rights to this title, please refer to your licensing agreement for important billing and credit requirements.

THE ARGUMENT was originally produced by The Vineyard Theatre in New York City in May, 2005. The Artistic Director was Douglas Aibel. The performance was directed by Maria Mileaf, with sound and music by Obadiah Eaves and lighting by David Lander. The cast was as follows:

SOPHIE . . . . Melissa Leo

PHILLIP . . . . Jay O. Sanders

HERB . . . . John Othman

THE ARGUMENT was produced by Theatre J in Washington DC on October 23, 2013. The performance was directed by Shirley Serotsky, with scenic design by Robbie Hayes, lighting by Martha Mountain, sound by Eric Shimelonis, and costumes by Erin Nugent. The cast was as follows:

SOPHIE . . . . Susan Rome

PHILLIP . . . . James Whalen

HERB . . . . Jefferson A. Russell

CHARACTERS

SOPHIE – EARLY FORTIES; A SUBSTANTIAL WOMAN AND ARTIST.

Charming. Her warmth, humor and sensuality are the first thing one notices about her, though her beauty could hardly be overlooked. Grounded by her commitment to her life's work, she is complex but not neurotic. Whatever challenges and obstacles she's faced have given her a strong and generous sense of herself, all of which are immediately appealing, especially to Phillip, who is a wise judge of character. They are a good match for one another. Their attraction is palpable, real and they offer one another the kind of relationship each still quietly hoped for, but never expected.

PHILLIP – LATE FORTIES; A SUBSTANTIAL AND APPEALING MAN AND BUSINESSMAN.

Phillip is a man's man, in that he has a modest, non- abrasive confidence which inspires trust and friendship in most people that he meets. He is utterly reliable and loyal and expects that of others. He says what he means and means what he says. He has a knack for business which was his driving passion for years, although, at this stage of his life he is spending more time in reflection than he once did. He is at a turning point of sorts and meeting Sophie compliments his desire to experience life more potently and purely. Her vibrance reinvigorates him and with Sophie he feels more present and hopeful than ever before.

HERB – FORTIES OR FIFTIES; A BENIGN AND WELL-INTENTIONED COUPLES THERAPIST.

Herb has made good communication his life's work. He really believes that the world would be better, safer and more humane if people practiced good communication skills. His methodology is based on Harville Hendricks' Amago technique, which is often described to couples as "compassion in action". He's ever hopeful that teaching couples this therapeutic paradigm will win the day. When couples do not benefit from working with him he feels that he has personally failed.

TIME

Now.

AUTHOR'S NOTE

The / or slash mark indicates where overlapping dialogue begins.

For B with love

Scene One

(It is dark. A door opens onstage. A man and a woman enter through the open door into **PHILLIP**'s *studio apartment. They are kissing. They walk-kiss through the room towards the bed. It is passionate, but it is not overwrought made-for-the-movies passion. This is truer and perhaps more awkward, interrupted by an unexpected piece of furniture or an unwieldy piece of clothing. They end up in an oversized easy chair. Lights fade – end of scene.)*

Scene Two

(A few hours later. **SOPHIE** *stirs. She slips on something nearby before emerging from the bed.* **PHILLIP** *rolls over and turns on bedside lamp.)*

SOPHIE. *(Self-conscious, exposed, not sure what to say)* This isn't a common occurrence for me.

PHILLIP. Me either.

SOPHIE. Really?

PHILLIP. Yes. Seriously.

SOPHIE. I don't really know you well enough to believe you. Oh god.

(This moment can't help but feel awkward.)

Excuse me. I'm a little thirsty.

(She ventures timidly towards the open kitchen.)

PHILLIP. Check the fridge.

SOPHIE. *(She has trouble opening the refrigerator door.)* I can't seem to open it.

PHILLIP. *(as he heads offstage to the bathroom)* Give it a yank. Apologies in advance. Not sure you'll find much in there.

SOPHIE. *(She pulls opens the refrigerator door, examining contents.)* Wow. You were right.

PHILLIP. *(offstage)* I warned you.

SOPHIE. You keep Cheerios in the fridge? Interesting.

PHILLIP. *(offstage)* I keep *everything* in the fridge. That way nothing goes bad.

SOPHIE. There are five kinds of cereal in here.

PHILLIP. The American Way. Five choices of virtually the same thing. It's my go-to-meal.
Now *I'm* embarrassed.

SOPHIE. *(examining contents)* Let's see. One head of lettuce. One stick of butter. Eggs. Milk.

PHILLIP. Check the date. (**PHILLIP** *emerges from the bathroom.)*

SOPHIE. And really cold bananas.

PHILLIP. A man and his fridge.

SOPHIE. *(picking up a bottle)* And what's this? A single bottle of curry powder?

PHILLIP. That's been there a while.

SOPHIE. Something tells me there's a story attached to this little bottle of spice.

PHILLIP. Well. Let's see, someone tried to cook for me.

SOPHIE. Bowls?

PHILLIP. Cabinet on the left.

SOPHIE. *(as he approaches her, sort of staring)* What are you doing?

PHILLIP. Watching you.

SOPHIE. Oh. Is that good? I suddenly feel enormous pressure to move about in a charming way.
Don't look too closely.

PHILLIP. I already have.

SOPHIE. Oh, yeah, right. God. I'm nervous. And, you're very – what?

PHILLIP. What?

SOPHIE. Relaxed.

PHILLIP. You have a lot to do with it.

(He approaches her, hoping to make her more comfortable. He kisses her tenderly.)

You know, I like you in my kitchen.

SOPHIE. *(She slips away, sheepish.)* Oh, I don't want you to get the wrong impression.

PHILLIP. About what?

SOPHIE. About me and kitchens.

PHILLIP. *(He laughs, enjoying her.)* I see. You don't like to cook?

SOPHIE. Well, I like to *eat*, but I don't exactly think of myself as a "preparer" of food.

PHILLIP. *(He heads back to the bed.)* Come back.

SOPHIE. I'm looking for silverware.

(*finding it*)

I prefer eating out.

PHILLIP. I see.

SOPHIE. (*preparing two bowls of cereal and milk*) Milk or plain?

PHILLIP. Milk.

SOPHIE. But I am, you know, what's the word?

PHILLIP. Particular?

SOPHIE. I like simple food prepared well. And I have favorites. Salads. Pasta. In fact, I'm a pasta...
what's the word?

PHILLIP. Enthusiast?

SOPHIE. No. It's more utilitarian than that.

PHILLIP. Oh.

SOPHIE. I used to eat a plate of pasta every day.

PHILLIP. Every single day!

SOPHIE. I developed a taste for it in grad school, when I was poor. Well, I'm not *not* poor, especially by some standards. What was I saying?

PHILLIP. You're a Pasta...Proletariat.

SOPHIE. I love it, unless of course, it's overcooked. Over boiled.

PHILLIP. *Par-boiled.* Don't they do that in restaurants?

SOPHIE. Par-boiled. That's an undefendable sin!

PHILLIP. A "pasta" sin.

SOPHIE. (*She heads back to bed, cereal bowls in hand.*) See, I don't care if you call it macaroni or noodles or eat it cold or cut it with a knife even –

PHILLIP. (*He follows her to the bed.*) Oh, you *are* forgiving.

SOPHIE. But if you don't cook it *al dente* –

PHILLIP. Forget it. Toss it. It's history.

SOPHIE. Exactly. Cheers.

(*They clink bowls or spoons before eating. They chew in silence for a minute.*)

PHILLIP. The curry powder belonged to my ex-wife, Pamela.

SOPHIE. Pamela.

PHILLIP. I mean, it was ours until she…let me have it.

SOPHIE. I see.

PHILLIP. We were separating. I moved in here and she came over to make us a meal. Indian food. A feast to put things right.

SOPHIE. Was she draped in purple silk and wearing little whaddyacallems on her fingers?

PHILLIP. Cymbals?

SOPHIE. Cymbalettes? A fun little belly dance or something?

PHILLIP. No. We fought while everything burned.

SOPHIE. I see. One wife?

PHILLIP. Yes. *Yes!*

SOPHIE. Everyone has a past, right?

PHILLIP. Hopefully.

SOPHIE. Right.

(They eat, after a moment.)

So, um, why'd you marry her in the first place?

PHILLIP. Why did I marry her? I loved her.

SOPHIE. Well, that's a good answer. How long were you married?

PHILLIP. Almost six years. Together for eight.

SOPHIE. And, then what happened?

PHILLIP. What happened?

SOPHIE. I mean was it a sudden sort of thing – do you mind my asking, I'm just –

PHILLIP. Looking for clues?

SOPHIE. Too many questions? Sorry.

PHILLIP. Not at all.

SOPHIE. I guess I'm checking if it's safe.

PHILLIP. *(He finds this amusing)* If it's safe? If *I'm* safe?

SOPHIE. Well, no offence. It's just that I've just broken *all* the dating safety tips I have posted on my refrigerator.

PHILLIP. I see. Rules of the road.

SOPHIE. Rule #1: No alcohol on the first three dates.

Rule #2: No sex on the first three dates –

PHILLIP. Oops.

SOPHIE. – And Rule #3,

(He kisses her.)

I can't remember.

PHILLIP. *(She kisses him – it's tender.)* It's good to have rules, isn't it?

SOPHIE. I remember. Rule #3: Listen and learn. My grandmother used to tell me: "Sophie, don't be Johnny Carson *and* the guest. Mouth closed, ears open."

PHILLIP. Johnny Carson. There's a throwback.

(He laughs.)

SOPHIE. Do you have children?

PHILLIP. No. We were too busy *working* on our relationship. You?

(She shakes her head.)

What about your work, your profession? You said you were a painter.

SOPHIE. Yes. You? What do you do, finance, wasn't it?

PHILLIP. Trader. Commodities.

SOPHIE. A gambler, right.

PHILLIP. Well, actually, that's, that's the part that started to wear me out. All day, all week, all those years, I was either winning or losing, and it got so that everything in between started to seem pointless.

SOPHIE. Scary.

PHILLIP. Yeah. Then, about 18 months ago my father died. Rough. I could feel my edge, my adrenaline for trading waned. And then…they let me go.

SOPHIE. I'm so sorry.

PHILLIP. Don't be. Turned out to be the best thing really. I'd saved some money. Made some good investments over the years. So I left the city for a little island in Maine. Monhegan Island, where I joined a…middle-aged rowing club. Sat under a tree, books, naps.

SOPHIE. Sounds pretty good.

PHILLIP. Simple pleasure. I'd forgotten simple pleasure was even an option.

SOPHIE. Pleasure. Oh God. I think I'm too worried about the world to feel pleasure. Maybe it's also, you know, living in New York City. That particular brand of striving and loud opinion.

So, where's your dog?

PHILLIP. My dog? Oh. Well, we sort of share her. I take her when Pamela goes away.

SOPHIE. But you said you had to leave the party to walk her.

PHILLIP. *(apologetically)* Oh yeah, well, it was kind of a line.

SOPHIE. *(horrified)* A line? A pick-up line?

PHILLIP. It was so loud at the party. I just wanted to get us out of there.

SOPHIE. I fell for a pick up line.

I can't believe it! I'm so ashamed.

PHILLIP. Don't be ashamed.

SOPHIE. *(playfully)* Ashamed of you!

(She kisses him. Their chemistry is apparent.)

You're not a beast in disguise are you?

PHILLIP. You've had experience with beasts?

SOPHIE. Maybe beast is too strong a word – Well, we wouldn't really qualify for true adulthood if we hadn't been driven slightly mad by the "wrong" man…or the "wrong" woman, would we?

PHILLIP. No, we certainly wouldn't.

SOPHIE. Mine was only half beast anyway. Quarter beast, really, to be fair.

PHILLIP. Three quarters man.

SOPHIE. Nearly. Let's just say he was high strung.

PHILLIP. I see. No good qualities?

SOPHIE. Great painter. That was his whole life.

PHILLIP. Husband?

SOPHIE. *(affirmative)* Hmm hmm.

(**PHILLIP** *holding her hand, noticing paint in the lines of her palm and nails:*)

PHILLIP. Wow. Look at your hands!

SOPHIE. I ran out of turpentine.

PHILLIP. When were you painting?

SOPHIE. Everyday, nearly. Sometimes for 14, 15 hours at a time.

PHILLIP. Hmm, I'm impressed.

SOPHIE. The whole process of making a painting *happen* takes time. It's got its highs and lows, but I guess I like that. Any painting, any *good* painting is evidence of a struggle, and well, when I'm caught, when I'm in the thick of it –

(**PHILLIP** *holding her hand, enchanted*)

I feel a kind of relief. I dunno. It's hard to explain.

PHILLIP. What color is that?

SOPHIE. That is, let's see, Prussian Blue.

PHILLIP. That?

SOPHIE. Cinnabar Red.

PHILLIP. Cinnabar.

SOPHIE. Oxidia Brown. I guess you could say I collect color.

PHILLIP. I've known women who collect scarves, shoes, *men*.

SOPHIE. Don't get me wrong. I collect shoes too!

PHILLIP. You're refreshing.

SOPHIE. *(blushingly)* Oh God. Am I? Aren't I – too old to be refreshing?

PHILLIP. You're kidding.

SOPHIE. No.

(She can't mask her vulnerability.)

PHILLIP. I was watching you at the party. Staring at you for at least an hour.

SOPHIE. *(nearly giddy)* No! Staring, really? What was I doing?

PHILLIP. Not staring back.

SOPHIE. Oh. Sorry, I'm not that much of a party person. If it hadn't been her birthday –

PHILLIP. Then, all of a sudden, you got up and I, I lost sight of you and panicked.

SOPHIE. *(bemused)* Yeah. Sure.

PHILLIP. I thought you'd left. But then, you came back with cake. A *huge* slice of chocolate cake!

SOPHIE. Oh God.

PHILLIP. A hunk, really.

SOPHIE. You saw that?

PHILLIP. And you ate it with such excitement, such appetite!

SOPHIE. Oh god – I'm so embarrassed.

PHILLIP. Spaghetti and cake. A woman after my own heart.

SOPHIE. I noticed you too.

PHILLIP. You did?

SOPHIE. Earlier. Before the cake.

PHILLIP. Why didn't you, you know, smile or wave or say something?

SOPHIE. I figured you must be taken.

(beat – simply)

I'm forty-two.

PHILLIP. I'm forty-nine.

(Lights fade – end of Scene 2.)

Scene Three

(Nearly one year later. Early evening. They are in his apartment which they now share. Subtle more "bohemian" changes are visible. A few accomplished paintings of hers decorate the walls.)

(The light is dim. We hear keys turning in the door. **PHILLIP** *enters with a small suitcase.)*

(He is well-dressed in a suit, tie, and trench coat.)

PHILLIP. SOPH!!!

SOPHIE. *(offstage)* Phillip!

PHILLIP. I'm home.

SOPHIE. Is that you??

PHILLIP. I think so, yes.

SOPHIE. You're not supposed to be here!

PHILLIP. I...I live here.

SOPHIE. Don't move.

PHILLIP. Don't move? Can I put my keys down?

SOPHIE. Close your eyes. I thought you were coming back tomorrow. I have a surprise.

PHILLIP. A surprise? How exciting.

SOPHIE. Close your eyes. Are they closed?

PHILLIP. They're closed.

SOPHIE. You promise they're closed.

PHILLIP. Promise and swear.

*(***SOPHIE*** enters wearing her "painting" clothes. She puts her hands over his eyes and kisses him.)*

PHILLIP. Hmmm. How nice.

SOPHIE. Hello there. No peeking.

PHILLIP. Hello.

SOPHIE. I have a surprise. An anniversary surprise.

PHILLIP. Did I forget something?

SOPHIE. It's 10 months tomorrow.

(With her hands gently over his eyes, she leads him towards the kitchen area)

SOPHIE. Did you find my card?

PHILLIP. I did. It was beautiful. Made me feel very lucky.

SOPHIE. I meant every word. This way. Don't open your eyes until I say.

(Stands back and gestures.)

You can open them.

(Seeing their new refrigerator – a vision – they are both a lit. Like two newlyweds.)

PHILLIP. Wow.

SOPHIE. I know.

PHILLIP. Wowee!

SOPHIE. I sold a painting. Bought us a fridge.

PHILLIP. Congratulations!

SOPHIE. Isn't it wild?

PHILLIP. It's great. It's big.

SOPHIE. I know.

PHILLIP. It's impressive.

SOPHIE. I know. Is it too much stainless steel for the room?

PHILLIP. No, no, not at all.

SOPHIE. It's handsome, isn't it?

PHILLIP. It's a…"VIKING".

SOPHIE. I feel like we should salute it or something.

PHILLIP. It's a big day, Soph.

SOPHIE. I know. A big fridge!

PHILLIP. *Our* fridge. I'm very happy for us.

SOPHIE. Me too.

(They kiss.)

Look inside.

(He opens it. It is pristine and almost totally empty.)

PHILLIP. It's cold. That's good.

SOPHIE. And look how bright it is. You could read a book in there it's so bright. And look at all these shelves and little compartments and look at all this storage.

Oh and this. Look at this. This is fantastic.

(opening one of the drawers)

See this. They call this a "crisper."

PHILLIP. What's it for?

SOPHIE. It's for crisping. Oh, don't touch that. It's raw pigment. I meant to bring it to the studio. It does better when it's cold.

PHILLIP. This really is an occasion! Our first big purchase.

SOPHIE. Now it's serious.

PHILLIP. Yup. It sure is. Wait. Something's missing.

SOPHIE. I know. Don't tell me.

(They look at each other-enjoying this rather obvious discovery)

PHILLIP. Food.

SOPHIE. Food!

PHILLIP. Food to eat.

SOPHIE. You are so right. Food for our fridge. Let's make a, you know...

PHILLIP. A list?

SOPHIE. Yeah. A list.

PHILLIP. A list of items.

SOPHIE. Food items, to commemorate the occasion of our new fridge.

PHILLIP. Now we are really committed to each other.

SOPHIE. Where's my pencil?

PHILLIP. Here.

(hands her a pencil)

SOPHIE. *(giddy, getting a pad too)* This is so scary.

(He sits. She may sit in his lap at anytime.)

PHILLIP. OK. Ready?

SOPHIE. Okey dokey, I'm ready –

(writes)

"Food List". Alright. You open the fridge and you see which happy, hearty, foody things?
Mouth watering what? First thing that comes to mind.

PHILLIP. Um. Cheese.

SOPHIE. Alright

(She writes.)

"Cheese".

PHILLIP. A selection of cheeses.

SOPHIE. Feta cheese, I love feta, and, and –

PHILLIP. And goat cheese –

SOPHIE. Feta *is* goat cheese.

PHILLIP. And that other one, the creamy one –

SOPHIE. Camembert. Brie de Meaux. Pot cheese. I love pot cheese.

PHILLIP. And the other cheese, from Vermont, you know, you know, the famous one – The one you eat with apples –

SOPHIE. Cheddar.

PHILLIP. *Sharp* cheddar.

SOPHIE. *(writes)* "Cheddar." Oh, and that other one from from Spain…it's blue, you eat it with pears and beer –

PHILLIP. Beer. Write down beer.

SOPHIE. Oh, it's so good. It's not Stilton, it's softer.

PHILLIP. Brie?

SOPHIE. Cabrales! Wait 'til you try that.

PHILLIP. Ok, that's enough cheese.

SOPHIE. What goes with cheese?

PHILLIP. Fruit.

SOPHIE. Melon. Plums. Grapes. Red.

(writes)

"Red grapes"

PHILLIP. Cold grapes in the middle of the night.

SOPHIE. I'll just write fruit.

> *(writes)*

> "Fruit".

PHILLIP. And juice.

SOPHIE. Mango and, and cranberry and –

PHILLIP. Orange juice for breakfast –

SOPHIE. *(writing)* "Orange juice". And grape juice! I love grape juice.

PHILLIP. And sliced whatsthatcalled…very thin.

SOPHIE. Welch's. Remember that?

PHILLIP. Prosciutto. And melon.

SOPHIE. *(writes)* "Welch's". This is so exciting.

PHILLIP. And Roast Beef.

SOPHIE. *(writing)* "Roast Beef". Got it. And, and smoked salmon, the really oily kind, not the Scottish, with a little lemon and what are those things, they come in bottles –

PHILLIP. Yoo-hoo.

SOPHIE. Capers!

PHILLIP. I love Yoo-hoo. Put down Yoo-hoo.

SOPHIE. And we'll get some of that black bread to go with the salmon – that thick, you know which one I mean –

PHILLIP. And butter.

SOPHIE. I love butter.

PHILLIP. Bread and butter.

SOPHIE. Oh God. Bread and butter.

PHILLIP. This is making me hungry!

SOPHIE. Me too. Let's have sex.

PHILLIP. Just like that. Wow.

> *(He winces as she climbs out of his lap.)*

> Ooh.

SOPHIE. What's wrong??

> *(As he's getting up, an ache.)*

PHILLIP. Ooh. Ooch. Cramp.

(She tears the blankets off the bed as he approaches. Waits for him there, all charm.)

SOPHIE. Nice to be home, isn't it?

PHILLIP. I'll say.

SOPHIE. I forgot. How was the interview?

PHILLIP. Fifty-fifty. Not sure I want it.

SOPHIE. I don't think I've ever seen you in that suit.

PHILLIP. This one? Sure you have. It's my interview suit.

SOPHIE. Phillip, you look so *alluring* in that suit.

*(**PHILLIP** starts to remove the jacket.)*

No, leave it on.

(A cell phone begins to ring and ring.)

SOPHIE. *(He takes off his shoes.)* Is it yours or mine? Can you tell?

PHILLIP. It sounds like yours.

(He starts to take off his suit jacket.)

SOPHIE. Shoot, sorry. Wait. Don't get undressed!

PHILLIP. *(putting it back on; game)* Okay.

SOPHIE. Oh Phillip, I don't want to get it, I swear I don't, but if it's whatshername. Blowhard.
Let me just see.

(She looks at the phone for the caller's number.)

Oh shoot. It's blowhard. I've just gotta –

PHILLIP. Who?

SOPHIE. Brigit Harding. The curator from the gallery. Don't move!

PHILLIP. Don't move?

(She answers her phone, overenthusiastic.)

SOPHIE. Hi, Brigit. Thanks for getting back.

(Motioning to him that she won't be long.)

SOPHIE. Uh huh. Yeah. I did.

*(**PHILLIP** starts to remove his tie.)*

*(to **PHILLIP**)*

Leave it on. Leave it on.

(into the phone)

Uh huh. Uh huh.

*(holding the phone against her hand, to **PHILLIP**)*

I want to make love to you in that suit.

(into phone)

Uh huh. Uh huh. I saw that too.

(He starts to whistle in anticipation.)

And I had one thought.

(She motions for him to keep his "whistling" down.)

I guess I miss the the color we'd originally discussed, because now, the impression I'm getting is well, I dunno, kind of grim, you know, which I'm, I'm sure you don't intend at all.

(He might return to the refrigerator again, while she becomes thoroughly drawn into the demands of the phone call, pacing the floor as she talks quickly.)

Well, yes, one can see them, *dimly*, but who wants to see anything that way? The wall color, in my opinion, should, should just be white. Plain old, you know, white!

*(Makes a disagreeable and exhausted face re: Brigit to **PHILLIP** who is still anticipating the end of the phone call.)*

I hear you but I, I just don't understand the choice for for grey…because, how are they going to be able to interpret any of what you just said in the Goddamn dark, you see what I mean? …I'm not criticizing your decision, I mean, I just want to see if we can revisit – Brigit – Can you hear me? Brigit??? Hello? Shit.

PHILLIP. What happened?

SOPHIE. Either she's just gone inside the Midtown Tunnel or she hung up on me. I think she may actually have hung up on me! Can you believe it? What did I say? Did I overfawn or underfawn?

PHILLIP. A little of both.

SOPHIE. "What do I mean by grim?!" That's what she just asked me!! What do I mean? I mean, *bad*, Brigit!! Grey and dark and hideous and bad! I don't care who she is, I can't not be honest about it! It's my work!

PHILLIP. You said Goddamn.

SOPHIE. I did?

PHILLIP. "Goddamn dark." That's what you said.

SOPHIE. Well, I wanted to say "fucking dark" but I resisted.

PHILLIP. In some circles "Goddamn" is worse.

SOPHIE. Really?

PHILLIP. You sounded angry.

SOPHIE. I did? I mean, I *was* angry, but I shouldn't *sound* angry.

PHILLIP. Right.

SOPHIE. That'll just –

PHILLIP. Yeah –

SOPHIE. What should I do? Should I call her back?

(looking for the phone)

Where's my phone?

PHILLIP. Call her later.

SOPHIE. She tells me she's, she's "culling a mood'. Creating a "hook". You know what that means, don't you?

PHILLIP. What?

SOPHIE. It means I'm at the mercy of a lot of crap, Phillip!

PHILLIP. Maybe it'll be lucky crap.

SOPHIE. I've seen lucky crap.

PHILLIP. And?

SOPHIE. This looks like *un*lucky crap. Christ! A hook!

(dialing)

A bloody meat hook is what!

PHILLIP. C'mere.

SOPHIE. And I'll be hanging from it. I'm the painter and she's offended. I hate that. Christ!

Straight to voicemail!

PHILLIP. Does this mean you're not going to undress me?

SOPHIE. *(worried)* This isn't what I'm good at. Handling people like her. The "It-Girl" Curator in Louboutin and Prada.

(He exits into the bathroom – she talks after him.)

And you know what's worse?! The guy showing with me- the Romanian guy, really good artist, these large encaustic panels, so he comes by takes one look at his part of the exhibit, and lets her have it! Tells her "THE LIGHT IS SHIT! I WILL SUFFER FROM THIS FUCKINK AMERICAN SHIT!"

And then she says to him, in this out-of-the-clear-blue-kitty-cat voice.

(We hear water – he's taking a shower.)

"You're right, Davron. It's too dark. You need more light! Of course you do!" And guess what? He'll get light and I won't.

(calling Brigit's number again)

Because he can say "fuck" and I can't say "Goddamn." And I didn't even mention the problem of thematic flow painting to painting - Which, of course, she hasn't given one thought to. Or maybe she has, which is worse.

(continuing into phone – her "pleasant" voice)

"Hi there Brigit, I think we just got cut off. I'm home. Bye."

(Dives under the pillow, temporarily overwhelmed, then, emerging and calling out:)

Phillip? Sweetie? Where are you? Come back. Is your suit still on?

(**PHILLIP** *enters eagerly. Almost excited. He is dripping wet with a towel around his waist, and holding a pregnancy test in his hand.*)

PHILLIP. Soph?

SOPHIE. What?

PHILLIP. Sophie. Honey. This.

SOPHIE. *(remembering)* Oh. God. I forgot.

PHILLIP. Why didn't you tell me?

SOPHIE. Oh God, Phillip. I was going to tell you. Of course. I was so surprised to see you and then the call...

PHILLIP. *(happy)* This is...

SOPHIE. Yes, but but those things can be wrong, you know. I thought I'd do it again to be sure.

PHILLIP. Amazing.

SOPHIE. I'll go to the Doctor tomorrow.

PHILLIP. How many weeks?

SOPHIE. I'm not sure. Four.

(beat, unsure)

Five.

(beat)

Six.

(Her cell phone begins to ring. Lights fade – end of scene 3.)

Scene Four

(A few days later.)

(**SOPHIE** *is preparing pasta and salad for dinner.* **PHILLIP** *mid-story, speaking at a clip.*)

PHILLIP. So, when I showed up Howie said he needed a fourth for this tournament thing. He's the oil cracks guy.

SOPHIE. Who lost all his money during the crash and made it back ten times over?

PHILLIP. Brilliant guy. And Jeff Touey is with us-

SOPHIE. The "bonds" guy who keeps asking you to work with him.

PHILLIP. Cut up. Prankster. Known him for years. So, it's me and Howie Weinstein –

SOPHIE. And Jeff Touey –

PHILLIP. Right, and Ricky Rasher, S&P guy, compulsive, neat freak, and as Willow Ridge Greens Committee Chairman, it's his job to to be overseer for the condition of the course, which he takes *very* seriously.

SOPHIE. All this is the setup, right?

PHILLIP. Right, ok, so, Jeff Touey – You know, you met him at that Halloween party last year –

SOPHIE. The guy wearing diapers with the bow and arrow?

PHILLIP. Cupid, right. Irish from the Bronx, great wife, kids –

SOPHIE. I remember.

PHILLIP. Lost untold brain cells in the nineties, coke, straightened out, and all he wants out of life is a good laugh.

SOPHIE. Got it. Howie, Ricky, Jeff.

PHILLIP. Right, so, we're at this gorgeous course in Palm Beach, and Touey buys this stuff from the airport shop – a little item called "Smelly Can of Shit".

SOPHIE. *(good naturedly)* Lovely. Lovely.

PHILLIP. Which, apparently, dispenses a substance in a shaving cream like manner, but has the appearance and smell of an actual human turd.

SOPHIE. Maybe you should save this story for after dinner?

PHILLIP. So we get to the club and on the first tee Touey shows me and Weinstein the little can of smelly stuff and outlines his plot to drive Rasher nuts.

(*She is multitasking between the pasta, sala. He brings the salad to the table, helping her as he tells the story.*)

SOPHIE. I haven't tossed that yet.

PHILLIP. So, we're playing, it's the third hole, and Rasher hits his ball off to the right in the rough.

SOPHIE. Uh huh.

PHILLIP. Meanwhile, the other guys drive up ahead in their golf cart, allegedly to find Rasher's ball and of course, when they find it, Touey sprays out a little pile of, you know, "Shit in a Can", about three inches in front of the ball and then they, quick, drive off to hit their own shots about twenty yards away. So, a coupla minutes go by until Rasher sees the stuff and shouts out, "Hey, what the hell is this?" And Touey, all innocent, says "Oh my god, it looks like someone took a shit out here!"

You know, it's like one of the most prestigious clubs around there, so Rasher says "It must have been a dog from the neighborhood," Then Weinstein, being an an outdoorsman and *noted Jewish hunter*, walks over to inspect the pile and says, "Hey, that doesn't look like animal shit to me, that's *human* excrement!" And Rasher's, like, "Who the hell would take a dump in the middle of my course? Who the hell would do that???" And we're telling him relax, hit his shot and just forget it, you know –

SOPHIE. Uh huh. Uh huh.

PHILLIP. But the poor guy can't let it go, and when he goes to hit, naturally, he *flubs* his shot straight into the bunker in front of the green – takes *two* shots to get out of the bunker and, swear to God, *three* putts for a, for a triple bogey.

SOPHIE. *(missing the agony of this entirely)* Sorry, a putt is what again?

PHILLIP. So, after the eighth hole, I'm with Rasher while Touey and Weinstein drive ahead to the next tee and spray *another* pile on the ninth tee box.

(SOPHIE hands the wine bottle and bottle opener to PHILLIP to open.)

Okay, so now we're all at the tee and Rasher walks up to hit and sees the the out-of-context addition on his perfectly manicured tee box, and he's like "What the fuck?"

SOPHIE. Could you open that sweetie?

PHILLIP. So, this time, we all, you know, confirm that it is, indeed, a repeat offence and definitely "man-made" to boot, and Ricky is, you know, he's going nuts, cursing, muttering, and when he goes to move the pile out of the way with his golf club, the Caddie screams out, "Hey, don't touch that with your club, man, I got to clean that sucker"

(PHILLIP finds this incredibly funny.)

And Ricky is beside himself, sweating, swearing –

SOPHIE. Yeah, you said.

PHILLIP. – and of course, needless to say, he tops his next shot, which dribbles thirty yards off the tee box and he's like, "fuck it!!", and hurls his club, which, which hits a tree and comes to rest with the the shaft at a sickening, but like perfectly bent ninety-degree angle!!

(more laughter, beat)

SOPHIE. Sounds like you guys had fun!

PHILLIP. Jeff literally bit his forearm to keep from cracking up. So, finally on the eighteenth hole –

SOPHIE. There's more?

PHILLIP. – while Rasher's putting out, Touey empties the last of the stuff right, right next to the accelerator of Weinstein's golf cart. And when Rasher sees it there, he, he finally puts it all together, turns back to us, you know, and we are –

(laughter)

– we are literally on our backs rolling on the green, hysterical.

SOPHIE. Dinner.

(They both sit at the table.)

PHILLIP. *(nearly out of breath)* Oh my God.

(suddenly remembering)

And the caddie was in on it, too, only I didn't know that! Jeff slipped him a twenty.

SOPHIE. I don't get it.

PHILLIP. You don't get what?

SOPHIE. *(Tossing the pasta – quiet, a beat. Something is irking her – what is it? She may not even know herself.)* I mean, I don't get what the whole golf craze is about? And the "club" thing.

PHILLIP. The club thing?

SOPHIE. I mean, "the joining" thing. It's just not in my frame of reference, I guess.

PHILLIP. Whaddya mean?

SOPHIE. Joining these over-the-top clubs where, where immigrant caddie slaves seem doomed to watch while mostly white men swipe madly at little bumpy balls –

PHILLIP. I was just telling a story, Soph.

SOPHIE. – hoping they'll bat them across great man-made expanses of chemical-soaked lawn – trekking from bitty hole to bitty hole.

(imitating, a bad Texas accent)

"Can I get the ball in the little hole…I hope I can!!"

PHILLIP. It's Florida, Soph, not Texas.

SOPHIE. Everyone, everywhere pining for the, the advantages that the "haves" have.

PHILLIP. *(concerned)* I think this is about something else.

SOPHIE. And I'm just wondering, is one of those advantages really GOLF?!? Cuz if it is...

(She begins to grate parmesan cheese over his plate of pasta.)

PHILLIP. I'm just trying to keep things a little light, you know.

SOPHIE. I mean, the rigorous and demanding process –

PHILLIP. *(RE: the cheese)* Thank you, that's enough.

SOPHIE. *(feeling defensive)* – of of making art is, personally, more –

PHILLIP. That's enough cheese.

SOPHIE. – more life-enhancing than, well, golf and fake shit in a can, that's all.

PHILLIP. NO MORE CHEESE!

(He places his napkin in his lap.)

Mind if I begin?

(He begins to eat. She tastes hers.)

SOPHIE. *(She pushes away her plate.)* It's overcooked.

(She leaves the room and slams the bathroom door. He pours himself a tall glass of wine, and patiently, drinks and eats. After a while she quietly re-enters, softened.)

PHILLIP. It's very good.

SOPHIE. I'm sorry. I'm very sorry.

PHILLIP. Sophie, honey, sit. I understand. We have a lot on our minds.

(She joins him at the table – vulnerable – she pours herself a glass of wine. Drinks some. He watches.)

SOPHIE. Yesterday, I went uptown to your sister's apt, to drop off your nephew's "belated" birthday present, and when I got there Petie started having a great big screaming meltdown, you know. They were headed to that jazz for toddlers music group and they were planning to walk thru central park on their way there so he could have the thrill of wearing his brand new light up sneakers that turn colors with every step, but apparently Beth couldn't find the sneakers anywhere and he wouldn't leave home without them. So me, your sister and her Ecuadorian housekeeper, we're down on all fours, looking, bending, searching everywhere for 30 minutes or more and finally, under a mountain of talking trucks and big plastic toys, Beth finds them. So now, she's rushing and there may not be time to walk thru the park to get to class, which Petie's not too happy about, but still, you know, she's triple tasking the way she does, gets his sippy cup, velcro's the little straps, puts on his coat, gets his hat, some mittens, the snaps, the zippers, I mean, I swear, it's 50 degrees outside and he's dressed for Antarctica! None of my business, I'm just standing there smiling, you know, trying to seem helpful and invisible at the same time – she's clearly stressed but determined to keep moving forward and then desperate, I guess, for adult English speaking company she invites me along to the jazz class. She thinks I'd get a kick out of it 'cuz it's Duke Ellington Day and they're going to pretend to ride a miniature "A" train – I mean, I want to get to the studio, but I'm feeling like I should go. Like she *needs* me to go, so, we're all finally out the door by the elevator; and Petie who's all hyped up from that blue slurpy surreal Gogurt crap forgets to mention to Beth that he has to go to the bathroom and, and so he just, you know, lets loose a little geyser, which flows like a rushing river down his pants' leg and develops into a mini-pee pool around his feet, which somehow...I dunno, short-circuits the flashing light in his sneakers. Well, he starts screaming, the top of his lungs, hiccupping with grief and and frustration and then, and then I did the worst thing, Phillip. The worst thing. I'm embarrassed to tell you.

PHILLIP. What?

SOPHIE. *(ashamed of her behavior)* When she hustled him back in the apartment to change him, I just…I just *ran* away. I haven't even called her to explain.

(She wells up. And now to the meat of the questions at hand)

We've had these few days apart.

PHILLIP. *(tender)* I know, I thought you needed time.

SOPHIE. I appreciated that. I did need some time. And since I got the news, not one minute has gone by that I wasn't thinking about it.

PHILLIP. Me too.

SOPHIE. I've been going over and over it and I – I still feel like I'm not ready to even know how to think about this.

PHILLIP. Who's ever ready? You know, we're not talking about a big family. We're only talking about one.

SOPHIE. I know, but, I really didn't even know that you wanted a child, Phillip.

PHILLIP. Me either. I mean, one way or another it just never seemed right. But now, it does.

SOPHIE. *(She wants to be sensitive and communicate thoughtfully. In preparation, she takes another sip of wine before she begins to speak.)* When my sister had her second child she said that a child…is like a, a, farm. Day in, day out. Life on a working farm. It's waking up every morning, crack of dawn, winter and summer, seven days a week to plant, till, sow, water and watch; alert to all the things that could ever possibly interrupt the, the harvest.

PHILLIP. *(softened by her "farm" metaphor)* That's beautiful. But plant and sow are the same thing.

SOPHIE. Every day, every hour of their life, it's the waxing, waning, lively needs of a little person.

PHILLIP. He'd sure be beautiful. She.

(Oops. He didn't get it. She takes another sip of wine, tries to explain herself another way.)

SOPHIE. *(still, with caution)* I'm afraid that could happen to me.

PHILLIP. You'll have me to help you.

SOPHIE. No. Children are gifts. No one can argue with that, of course. But I'm talking about that suddenly side-tracked life that Jenna and Beth and even my sister have chosen for themselves.

PHILLIP. I thought your sister made a choice to stop working until the kids were older.

SOPHIE. She's never going back to her career.

PHILLIP. *(bemused)* What career?

SOPHIE. She was a writer! She wrote novels, Phillip.

PHILLIP. Chapters. She wrote chapters.

SOPHIE. She was talented, passionate, engaging! I ask her how she is now; she says all she wants to do is sleep! All these kids screaming in the background!

PHILLIP. That's what kids do.

SOPHIE. *(entre nous)* And they bicker about the silliest, petty things now. Their marriage is all about the kids. And they never have sex anymore.

PHILLIP. Who? Jack and your sister?

SOPHIE. Beth and Warren! She told me. They made love *last* year!!

PHILLIP. We'll have sex, don't worry.

SOPHIE. Seriously, Phillip, children turn lovers into relatives. It's, it's not their fault, but they just do. And we're still at the beginning. When everything is "yes" and "why not?" I mean, we have love that's simple and easy –

PHILLIP. We do.

SOPHIE. Neither of us have ever had that before, right?

PHILLIP. Yes. Exactly.

SOPHIE. I was just thinking the other day that when we're not working, we can travel together, we can explore, go places we've wanted to go all our lives and now we can do all that together, I mean, you know where Beth goes –

PHILLIP. Stop with Beth.

SOPHIE. *(Incredulous. Can't help but speedily riff on the details of all that she's observed.)* She goes to Starbucks! While Petie naps in the stroller after all the fucking classes she drags him to, she goes to Starbucks on Columbus Avenue and sits there with all the other people, *without a job,* and, and drinks a six dollar cup of barbequed coffee with a tower of whipped cream and vanilla and caramel, opens her mini-iPad and shops online, obsessively, for all kinds of crap she so doesn't need! Click click click. I mean, PayPal is her best friend. And that's what she does for FUN – or to escape, who knows?

PHILLIP. You're working yourself up here, do you hear yourself?

SOPHIE. You're right, ok, I do that sometimes, but all of this has to be weighed in the balance of who we are now, doesn't it, because, well, frankly, I mean, I'd rather hang myself from a shower stall than be someone like Beth, posting mundane pictures everyday on her Facebook page and instagramming enhanced photos of the family's daily outings or worse, posting pictures of what they're eating and where!!

PHILLIP. Relax, you wouldn't be that kind of mother.

SOPHIE. He walked! He talked! Oh my God! Call Huff Post! I'm sorry, but to me, it's news if they *don't* walk! You know what I mean? If they never talk and say goo-goo, gaa-gaa their whole bloody life, that's something to talk about!

PHILLIP. When it's your own child –

SOPHIE. *(all her worst fears, she's beginning to pace)* He burped. He didn't burp. He pooped, he didn't. I don't see, I don't see how – I mean, the inevitable narrowing focus, the suddenly myopic objective of fortifying our little acre for our little family and how would I even be able to continue to paint?

PHILLIP. Sit down, you're pacing, for God's sake. We're just talking, Soph.

SOPHIE. *(back to him, tenderly)* It's not even a year since we met. Out of the blue blue sky, there's you, like a mirage, handsome and strong, but almost as quickly, this? Too quickly.

PHILLIP. Too quickly? You mean, you're thinking if it hadn't all happened so quickly –

SOPHIE. I'm thinking, I'm just too old to be having this problem.

PHILLIP. *(simply)* I wish you'd had that thought when you told me you couldn't get pregnant.

SOPHIE. *(defensive)* I didn't think I could. I've never been pregnant before and at my age it's an understandable assumption that it's never going to happen. I'm usually very careful, anyway, you know that.

PHILLIP. Alright, alright.

SOPHIE. So we made a mistake! Mistakes happen to everybody!

(Concerned, he takes away her glass of wine.)

Hey, hey, hey, Can I have my wine back, please!

PHILLIP. It's just – alright.

(Realizing he's overstepping, he hands it back.)

You're right. We're not kids having this problem. But, Soph, it's not worse because we're older. It's better.

SOPHIE. *(looking for the right words)* My body feels… ambivalent, at best.

PHILLIP. *You* feel ambivalent. Your body is doing what it's supposed to be doing under the circumstances.

SOPHIE. I don't know how to make a distinction between me and my body, Phillip. I don't think of it as separate from me. I mean, I don't know how to, how to, donate my body to something that I feel so –

PHILLIP. Alright, Sophie, I hear you.

SOPHIE. You do?

PHILLIP. I think so, yes.

(Pause – She ponders whether or not to say this. Moves in close to him. It feels, somehow, "wrong" to admit. Nearly a confession.)

SOPHIE. Phillip.

PHILLIP. What?

SOPHIE. Motherhood isn't a fantasy I have for myself.

PHILLIP. Never?

SOPHIE. Yes. Sure. But it changed.

PHILLIP. Just like that?

SOPHIE. Out of art school I was an intern with this amazing man, Issac Columbier, one of the best restorers of mostly 20th century art anywhere in the world and he began every new restoration by asking where the "secrets" were.

PHILLIP. What secrets?

SOPHIE. He believed that each painting had…privacies. Hidden layers of subtext and intention – and only when they were carefully deciphered and – and felt would he even begin the actual restoration work. His studio was – there were walls of, of antique cabinets, drawers with little brass handles filled with hundreds of tubes of paint, tins of gouache powders, another sort of pantry full of solvents and liniments. Little bricks of beeswax. Poultices made of black tea or tobacco leaf that he used to soften cracking paint. I swear, it was a wizard's pharmacy! And from six a.m. to three in the afternoon, four days a week, there he'd be, bent over one or another masterwork. I never knew who I would find there. A Dubouffet over here. In this corner, a small Cezanne! Opposite that, a Matisse. Then next month, Braque. Gauguin. I could get so close to them – I could smell the paint. Trace the the movement of the strokes; the unpretentiousness was so sexy; when I walked to work, I swear I felt like I was meeting a secret lover. But, one day, he called me very early in the morning, urgent, almost with the sound of fear in his voice and when I got to the studio he was just standing, sort of daunted, before a tall, broad canvas – a Bonnard, of a woman, a nude – I'd never seen anything shimmer like she did; whites, that seemed to be lit by candles, or was it the short strokes of pale yellow, set against the slightly longer strokes of what? What was that color made of? Even he couldn't figure it out. I stood beside him, the two of us, silent, until the sound of a passing siren broke in.

PHILLIP. Hmmm.

SOPHIE. *(moved by this memory)* Time stopped and he said that we were drawn into what Bonnard said was "the world before the wars began." It turned out we'd been standing there, looking, for 3 hours.

PHILLIP. You knew then.

SOPHIE. I had a clear, a very clear intention, and it wasn't… motherhood.

(Concerned, beat, fearful. She doesn't want to lose him over this.)

What are you thinking, Phillip?

PHILLIP. I don't know yet.

(She touches him. He doesn't move or looks away. Lights fade – end of Scene 4.)

Scene Five

(The next day)

(PHILLIP and **SOPHIE** *enter the upper west-side office of* **HERB**, *a couple's therapist.)*

HERB. And from the perspective of, let's say, higher consciousness, uh, human awareness is, well, limited. It's not that our view of reality which seems so pre-possessingly real is distorted, rather, it is merely the *reality* of *human* consciousness.

PHILLIP. *(trying to understand)* We think like humans? Is that what you're saying?

HERB. *(He laughs.)* Let's hope so. Let's think about, well, a bee, for example –

SOPHIE. A bumble bee?

HERB. Yes. A bumble bee has a different level of consciousness, in that its universe is made up of more elementary components such as, uh, heat, cold, softness, hardness, light, dark, etc. It's not that it has a *distorted* perception of the world as we know it, but more like it has a perfect "*bee*" perception of reality.

PHILLIP. Okay, so –

HERB. So, perhaps, and this is my point, that your response, Phillip, to the idea of Sophie's pregnancy –

PHILLIP. It's more than an idea.

HERB. Of course –

SOPHIE. I don't know why he keeps saying that. I think we both know it's more than an *idea.*

HERB. Hold on now, neither of your perceptions, of this situation is wrong or right, rather, it is the perfect "Phillip" perception of reality. And Sophie's sense of what to do next is the perfect "Sophie" perception of reality. Do you see what I mean?

SOPHIE. I think so.

PHILLIP. *(growing impatient)* I don't. I don't.

SOPHIE. What did you miss?

PHILLIP. What do you mean, "What did I miss?"

SOPHIE. Why are you asking me like that?

PHILLIP. Like what? I'm just asking.

HERB. Let me just point out here that Phillip didn't *miss* anything, it's just that his desire to have you agree with him on the issue of the pregnancy is probably preventing him from hearing you in the present.

PHILLIP. Hearing in the present? I'm listening to every word she's saying.

HERB. I said "hearing". There's a difference.

PHILLIP. *(impatience)* A difference between hearing and listening? I don't understand.

SOPHIE. Maybe you don't really *want* to understand. Sweetie, look how you're sitting. You seem distant.

PHILLIP. I'm just sitting here...am I sitting wrong?

HERB. Let's, let's –

PHILLIP. *(to* SOPHIE*)* I'm not sure I understand the logic of what he's getting at, that's all.

HERB. This is hard at first, I know.

SOPHIE. You don't understand the logic of what? My *feelings?*

HERB. *(bemused)* Hold on, now.

SOPHIE. It's just that he wants all my feelings to be logical.

PHILLIP. I want them to make *sense*, I mean, is that wrong too?

HERB. Whoa, whoa, whoa. I'd like to slow the pace of this down, because with any loaded issue, *momentum is not your friend.* It sparks a kind of self-righteous adrenaline that is particularly useless in the realm of conflict resolution, so, let's agree to try to pace ourselves much more deliberately, ok?

SOPHIE. Ok.

HERB. Phillip?

PHILLIP. Yes, but it's hard to slow down when you sense that you're in an emergency.

HERB. I thank you for saying that. I hear your anxiousness and your concern. But if you both don't slow down you may never address what you *"perceive"* as the emergency and *mortally wound* the capacity of the relationship to hold the contradictions here. Are you with me?

PHILLIP. More or less.

SOPHIE. Yes.

HERB. Your relationship is more than just the sum of two parts, there is *you*, Phillip. There is *you*, Sophie, and then there is the reality of a *third* entity, and I call it an entity because it is *alive* and *demanding* and *lush* and it is your *relationship*. And for the purpose of this session, *I* will represent your relationship. When something hurts the "relationship" I will say so. If alienating phrases ike "*he never*" or "*she always*" are said, I may gently point it out to you, or if we get ahead of ourselves I may choose to interrupt you with this bell.

(He removes a little bell from atop his side table and demonstrates. Not jokey, just a tool for this process.)

A little reminder to take a breath. Pull back the troops, that's all. Is that alright with you both?

SOPHIE. Ok.

*(**PHILLIP** nods.)*

HERB. Good. I like to think that this time with me is an exercise in compassion which might lead us out of the "argument" and into an atmosphere of more.

PHILLIP. More? More what? Can you be specific?

HERB. More love.

SOPHIE. That sounds hopeful.

PHILLIP. Ok.

HERB. Remember, the way one feels isn't necessarily the way it is.

PHILLIP. What does that mean? Sorry, it just sounds like so much crap. I'm not trying to resist the process here but I find things like that –

SOPHIE. But you are resisting.

PHILLIP. I'm being honest.

HERB. Sophie, try not to react to what Phillip says.

SOPHIE. But he always does that.

PHILLIP. I always do what?

HERB. Sophie. *Always* and *never*.

SOPHIE. Sorry.

HERB. Phillip? Go on. You were saying –

PHILLIP. I just don't, I just don't know if this is going to be use –

SOPHIE. Is going to be *what?*

PHILLIP. Never mind.

SOPHIE. Never mind?

PHILLIP. I said what I wanted to say.

SOPHIE. No, you didn't. You were about to but you / didn't.

PHILLIP. Well I thought better of it.

HERB. Phillip, can I entreat you to finish your thought?

PHILLIP. Well, uh, I don't actually remember it. I remember "never mind" but not what lead up to "never mind."

(beat)

HERB. *(noticing* **SOPHIE***)* Sophie?

SOPHIE. I just feel so hopeless when you say "never mind" like that.

PHILLIP. Well, I felt hopeless just trying to make sense of all this stuff.

HERB. Alrighty. Let's begin the exercise right here. Right where we are. Sophie, tell Phillip how you feel.

SOPHIE. How I feel?

HERB. Yes, tell him. 'You feel –'

SOPHIE. I felt hopeless when you –

HERB. Feel. Let's keep it in the present. It's more vulnerable to *feel* than to *have felt.*

*(***PHILLIP*** takes a deep breath.)*

Sophie, complete this sentence for me: I feel scared when you say "never mind" because –

SOPHIE. Um. I feel scared when you say "never mind" because I'm hoping we'll be able to solve our problem here, Phillip. I want that very much.

HERB. Yes, see, now that's already much less provocative, but still honest and more revealing, too. Want to add anything, Sophie?

SOPHIE. I think –

HERB. I feel.

SOPHIE. I feel that he's –

HERB. That "you're" – let's not speak in the third person.

SOPHIE. *(to* **PHILLIP***)* That you're sitting there thinking this whole thing is ridiculous and that is making me feel even more scared.

HERB. Scared of what exactly?

SOPHIE. Scared of…losing him.

(The absolute truth. **HERB** *looks toward* **PHILLIP***.)*

Losing you.

HERB. Great. Thank you. Now, Phillip, can you repeat what Sophie just said?

PHILLIP. Can I repeat it?

HERB. Literally repeat it, without commenting or reacting to it in any way. Just repeat the words, what you just heard Sophie say.

PHILLIP. *(looking at* **SOPHIE***)* You said that when I said the words "never mind" she felt, *you* felt scared.

HERB. Yes, and?

PHILLIP. Are you kidding?! I'm not allowed to say never mind?

HERB. Slow, slow. Phillip. In this case "are you kidding" is a provocative comment. Do you see?

PHILLIP. *(trying hard)* Yes. Yes, I do. Alright, forget "are you kidding" and forget "never mind." Forget them both. I don't know! What am I supposed to say?

SOPHIE. He's doing it.

HERB. Sophie.

SOPHIE. I didn't say "always."

HERB. It was implied. You were dissatisfied. You see how the misunderstanding begins…how it snowballs?

PHILLIP. Where is this going?

HERB. Bear with me. It's a process. Sophie has just told you she's afraid of losing you. Did you hear her?

(to **SOPHIE**, *tears falling from her eyes*)

There's tissue right there behind you.

SOPHIE. Thanks.

HERB. Did you hear what she said?

PHILLIP. Yes, yes I did.

HERB. Ok. Now, Phillip, can you complete this sentence: It makes sense to me that you would feel scared of losing me when I say "never mind" because –

PHILLIP. It doesn't make sense to me.

SOPHIE. It doesn't make sense to you?

HERB. But for the purpose of the exercise, Phillip, give this a try. "It makes sense to me, Sophie, because – "

PHILLIP. Um. It makes sense to me because, uh, because when I say "never mind" you interpret that as a sign of intractability, irritation and abandonment.

SOPHIE. Yes! Exactly! That's exactly right!!

HERB. Good, good.

SOPHIE. That's exactly what I'm feeling.

PHILLIP. I know.

HERB. That was great. Not so hard, was it?

PHILLIP. Not hard. Just *long*.

HERB. Until we get it under our belts the process may feel mechanical, but look at Sophie's face. How it's softened. You have just validated her experience of what you said. And that is loving and that warms the relationship and allows each person to balance or hold the argument, do you see, without needing to win it, and that simple *generosity* makes us each more flexible, and more available to encourage new ideas, new tendencies in one another, which is the fundamental purpose of relationships anyway and the only way to save the whole fuckin' world as far as I'm concerned.

PHILLIP. Is it my turn yet?

HERB. Yes. Yes it is.

PHILLIP. Well, I feel, uh, I feel very angry and this whole thing, frankly, is making me even angrier.

HERB. Hmm. Take a deep breath, Sophie. Can you repeat what Phillip just said, verbatim reporting, nothing more.

SOPHIE. What I heard you say is that you are feeling angry and that this is making you feel even angrier.

HERB. Did she get that?

PHILLIP. Yup.

HERB. Want to add anything to that?

PHILLIP. Nope.

HERB. Step 2. Sophie, complete this sentence: "It makes sense to me, Phillip, that you are feeling angrier and angrier because – "

SOPHIE. It makes sense to me, Phillip, that you are feeling angry and that you are getting even angrier because… we haven't even gotten down to the issue that brought us here in the first place.

(**PHILLIP** *nods – she got it*)

HERB. Very good. She got that. I'm your relationship and your relationship is feeling safe and attended to, right?

PHILLIP. I guess so, yes.

HERB. Step 3, and I really want you to use your imagination here, try to be generous. Sophie, complete this sentence: "I can imagine, Phillip, that you are feeling – "

SOPHIE. Um, I can, can imagine that you are feeling… frustrated, beyond belief, and frightened that you won't, *we* won't have time enough to figure all this out – I mean, if the last ten minutes is any indication of how long this process could take – I mean, I'd have to go and have the abortion before we actually got round to agreeing on an amicable solution.

HERB. Phillip?

PHILLIP. *(to* **SOPHIE,** *quietly)* What?

SOPHIE. *(to* **HERB)** Did I do it wrong?

HERB. Did she get that?

PHILLIP. *(threatened, to* **SOPHIE)** What did you say?

SOPHIE. What?

HERB. Easy does it.

PHILLIP. I see. Christ.

SOPHIE. What?!?

PHILLIP. Abortion? I mean, that's what all this is about? That's the amicable solution – an abortion?

HERB. Let's not react to words like "abortion".

PHILLIP. "Words *like* abortion"!

HERB. *(overlapping begins)* Let's back up.

SOPHIE. Well, if I don't go ahead with it –

PHILLIP. But we didn't ever talk about abortion!!

SOPHIE. *(to* **HERB)** How else am I *not* going to be pregnant, Phillip?

HERB. *(interjecting the best he can)* Let's slow down.

SOPHIE. *(to* **PHILLIP)** I didn't even realize children were this / important to you.

PHILLIP. You don't just drop the word into conversation! / You don't do that.

HERB. Your relationship is hurting.

PHILLIP. You never said it before now. / You never said that!

SOPHIE. Because I was thinking it through...

PHILLIP. Thinking what through? / The abortion.

SOPHIE. The possibilities, the options, I don't think / you've heard me, Phillip.

PHILLIP. You waited until we came here.

*(***HERB*** rings the bell softly to slow them down.)*

SOPHIE. Because I wanted, I wanted / to help prepare us...

PHILLIP. You said we were coming to discuss *all* the alternatives.

SOPHIE. All the alternatives to being pregnant? / How many other alternatives are there?

PHILLIP. Marriage, a real home! Not just to fucking "prepare" me, Sophie!

(**HERB** *rings the bell again gently.*)

HERB. Phillip. Sophie. Ow.

SOPHIE. *(to* **HERB**, *growing panic re:* **PHILLIP**'s *reaction)* I really don't understand what's happening.

PHILLIP. To finesse me in front of a therapist!

HERB. *(representing the relationship)* "Ow, ow!" I'm hurting.

SOPHIE. What's wrong with needing help with this?

HERB. May I interject?

PHILLIP. In front of a stranger!

SOPHIE. I wasn't finessing you. You're upset.

PHILLIP. I'm upset?!? Yeah, I'm upset!

HERB. Guys. Hello. Hey!

SOPHIE. I'm sorry. He's usually very – I think this may be about something else –

PHILLIP. Something else?!? It's about what it's about, Soph!

SOPHIE. *(gently)* About losing your father. The grief of that. I dunno.

PHILLIP. My *father!?*

HERB. Hold on...

SOPHIE. *(to* **HERB**, *grasping)* He died.

(*to* **PHILLIP**)

I don't know. Letting go of him.

PHILLIP. This isn't about my father, Sophie!

SOPHIE. *(to* **HERB***)* I don't know what to do!

HERB. Phillip – may I speak –

PHILLIP. *(to* **SOPHIE***)* This is about us!

(A direct threat. **HERB** *may ring the bell or not.)*

SOPHIE. *(emploring)* Exactly – which is why I wanted to come here in the first place!

PHILLIP. You know what this is –

HERB. Phillip, you have got to step back in order for your relationship / with Sophie to survive.

SOPHIE. We're here to find / a way to support us, that's all I wanted.

PHILLIP. Jesus Christ! This is an ambush.

HERB. Your relationship is hurting. / It's really hurting.

PHILLIP. Fucking ambush.

HERB. *(over their voices)* "I am wounded."

SOPHIE. I wanted to tell you in an atmosphere –

PHILLIP. Manage me in front of a stranger –

HERB. "I am very wounded."

SOPHIE. – that would favor us, that would help us through. / The opposite of an ambush actually.

PHILLIP. Pay some shrink 300 bucks an hour to hear bullshit that feelings aren't facts. / Here are the facts, OK?

SOPHIE. *(desperate)* Phillip, please.

PHILLIP. *(frightened, angry)* I want a choice. *I* want a choice!!!

HERB. Phillip.

*(***HERB*** *rings the bell.)*

PHILLIP. You never gave me a fucking second to even –

(As **HERB** *rings the bell to get their attention,* **PHILLIP** *slaps it out of his hand.)*

SOPHIE. *(wanting so badly to make sense to him, get through)* But how can I do that, how can I give you a choice? / Just tell me.

HERB. I just need you both to / stop reacting – please.

SOPHIE. I tried to explain my doubts, my fears.

PHILLIP. I deserve it. / I deserve it!

HERB. I know it's hard. / But if we can still try to model the process –

SOPHIE. Phillip. What are you doing?

PHILLIP. *(getting up to leave)* *(to* **SOPHIE***)* Thank you. / Thanks a lot!

HERB. *(imploringly, standing)* Let's not short-circuit the / opportunity we have –

SOPHIE. *(to* **PHILLIP***, strongly)* You can't leave now! / You can't.

PHILLIP. Fuck off, the both of you.

HERB. I want to encourage you not to leave / the room.

SOPHIE. I wanted to talk it through calmly, that's all.

PHILLIP. You want a *calm* abortion?

SOPHIE. Yes! Yes I do!

HERB. *(eager to rescue this session)* May I say something –

PHILLIP. Sorry. I'm not having a calm / abortion.

HERB. Can I suggest –

SOPHIE. Phillip –

PHILLIP. I'm not having any abortion!

SOPHIE. What are you talking about?

PHILLIP. And neither are you!

HERB. *(more strongly)* Could you sit down, please!

SOPHIE. *(finally owning her decision, through tears)* Yes, I am, Phillip. I made an appointment –

HERB. Could I just say –

PHILLIP. No!

SOPHIE. Yes!

PHILLIP. No!!

> *(He opens his wallet and throws three $100 bills on his chair.)*

HERB. Please, may I say something?

PHILLIP. It's not your fucking turn!

> *(***PHILLIP*** *leaves, a beat.)*

HERB. *(He's failed. To* **SOPHIE***.)* I'm so sorry…so sorry.

> *(Lights Fade – end of Scene 5.)*

Scene Six

(The next day. Night. **SOPHIE** *and* **PHILLIP***'s Apartment.)*

*(***SOPHIE*** is sitting up in bed eating ice cream from a Haagen-Dazs pint.* **PHILLIP***, sitting across the room. watching her intently.)*

PHILLIP. I'm sorry. Please talk to me.

(trying to find the right words)

I just want to –

(From his shirt pocket he removes a folded up card and reads.)

"And I knew to my feet and thru my heart that now is the richest time of my life." You wrote that, remember.

(She keeps eating, somewhat detached.)

"You have lifted my heart, flung it wildly into the air, and caught it surely, and now you hold it. And your holding it makes it pound more strongly and more softly than it ever pounded strongly or softly before."

SOPHIE. *(stoic)* I'm preparing for what I think is going to be a very difficult day.

PHILLIP. *(imploring)* It's not what we expected, or even what you want, I understand. But what if we take a chance together and just say "yes".

(She gets up and throws the pint of ice cream into the garbage. Sets her alarm clock.)

Sophie.

(She takes a pillow with her from their bed and sets herself up to sleep in the easy chair with make shift ottoman.)

Sophie.

(She turns off the light.)

Sophie.

(Lights Fade – end of Scene 6.)

Scene Seven

(Hours later, almost dawn)

(SOPHIE *is still asleep, however now, their bed sheet has been stripped from the bed and rather snugly tied around* **SOPHIE** *and the chair. It is not severely tight, but the way it wraps around her it oddly does the job of keeping her in the room.* **PHILLIP** *sits nearby, worried. He waits. Watches. Her alarm clock begins to beep. She wakes up.)*

PHILLIP. You are in no danger whatsoever. I promise, I do not want to hurt you. Sophie, I promise.

(beat)

I just need a little more time.

(She doesn't answer, he speeds up defensively, knowing he's acting irrationally.)

We all come to moments, crucial moments in our lives when we have choices, but depending on the situation, we might make the wrong choice, or make no choice at all, which could end up being the wrong choice.

SOPHIE. Your point?

PHILLIP. My point? I can't be the person who does nothing. Not when I think I know what to do.

SOPHIE. What to do. Tie me up?

PHILLIP. You're not really tied up, Sophie. Not really.

SOPHIE. I'm not?

PHILLIP. Not with rope. A sheet. I mean, I don't want to hurt you, Sophie.

SOPHIE. You said that already.

PHILLIP. I'm just trying to make an impression here.

SOPHIE. You have, trust me.

PHILLIP. I'm trying to make things make sense and it's all just moving a little too fast for me.

SOPHIE. So you tied me up?

PHILLIP. I wish you would stop saying that.

SOPHIE. Oww, my hand.

PHILLIP. C'mon, that doesn't hurt.

SOPHIE. Can I be the judge of that?

PHILLIP. Sophie, if if you want me to untie you, I will. Do you want me to untie you?

SOPHIE. Yes. Yes, I do. Does that surprise you?

PHILLIP. No, of course not.

> *(beat)*

I love you.

SOPHIE. I had a feeling you were going to say that.

PHILLIP. I do love you.

SOPHIE. "Do you say that to all the women you tie up?"

PHILLIP. Stop. I promise you, I have never done anything like this before.

SOPHIE. Oh, that's comforting.

> *(beat)*

PHILLIP. I know this is extreme.

SOPHIE. Yes.

PHILLIP. Even as I was doing it I was thinking, "this is extreme", but try to understand, bear with me.

SOPHIE. Do I have a choice?

PHILLIP. I was thinking of ways to try to delay this. Plans, plots. Another idea was to kind of kidnap you and take you on a sail for a coupla months.

SOPHIE. An ocean cruise. Wow, sounds romantic.

PHILLIP. Stop.

SOPHIE. You can't really expect a positive outcome from all this?

PHILLIP. I don't know what to expect.

SOPHIE. Hope for the best. Expect the worst!

PHILLIP. I just want…I just want you to think this through from a different perspective.

SOPHIE. *Your* perspective.

PHILLIP. It's just that I don't accept that you know what you're doing.

SOPHIE. I don't accept that *you* know what *you're* doing!

PHILLIP. *(reading again)* "You have lifted my heart, flung / it wildly into the air and caught it surely".

SOPHIE. Oh Christ – don't read it again, Phillip! Undo me!!

PHILLIP. Sophie! I'm a good catcher. You said so yourself. I'm a rare breed of capable fixers.

SOPHIE. *(sharply)* I don't want to be fixed.

PHILLIP. A helper. Have I ever even said "no" to you?

SOPHIE. *(emphatic)* I'm saying no to you. Finally, this is an unwanted pregnancy, and I am saying NO.

PHILLIP. Well, I hear you, but, but let me just say that "unwanted" doesn't actually describe the condition of the baby you're carrying –

SOPHIE. Ohh, please don't say that word.

PHILLIP. It only describes your attitude about it.

SOPHIE. I'm going to be late. Will you, will you pass me the phone?

PHILLIP. No. On principle. Sorry, I'm just committed to thinking it all the way through.

SOPHIE. What are you planning here, short of some kind of crime?

PHILLIP. Crime?!!! Oh Sophie, please.

SOPHIE. Yes. Yes. Keeping me here, against my will. People are waiting for me.

PHILLIP. *(hurt)* The *doctor*? I'm, what, I'm inconveniencing him?

SOPHIE. Her.

PHILLIP. Who is she to me? Who is she to you??? You're going to settle this with her and not me??

SOPHIE. Oh God. Will you just –

PHILLIP. *(pleadingly)* If you would just remember the, the qualities about me you fell in love with –

SOPHIE. *(incredulous) Now?* You want me to remember them now?!?

PHILLIP. One of them, whether you want to admit it or not, was that I know how to enjoy life. I do. I mean, let's face it, you were used to struggling through and I come along and I say, come with me, and let's live another way!

SOPHIE. Wait. You're talking about money?

PHILLIP. Not just money.

SOPHIE. I make a very decent living now.

PHILLIP. Yes, but you're so used to the little you've had, you still operate under it's rule, the rule of "no". Worry less about "career" stuff. Paint in your studio or better yet, come with me and, and paint on a hilltop in the South of France, an island in Greece.

SOPHIE. I don't need the comfort that your money brings.

PHILLIP. My money doesn't bring comfort Sophie. *I* bring comfort. That's what I'm saying.

SOPHIE. I couldn't do any of that with children.

PHILLIP. You get sitters and nannies / and you make things possible.

SOPHIE. I don't want nannies. Christ! I don't want to be PREGNANT!!!

PHILLIP. But you *are* pregnant. If you were more accustomed to the kind of love we have and had fewer hard-grained survival skills, you wouldn't automatically resist this. Fear this.

SOPHIE. I'm fearing you.

PHILLIP. *(insisting)* No, you're not.

SOPHIE. Yes, I am. I am!

PHILLIP. *(Hearing her, he unwraps the sheet from around her.)* All right, all right, then. Ok. Ok? I was just trying to –

(She leaves the room before he finishes his sentence. She returns quickly, putting on clothing as she gathers other things she needs: shoes, bag, etc.)

PHILLIP. *(hurting, desperate to save the relationship)* Let's not do this, let's not make hurting each other impossible to resist. It's just. I can't, I can't make the words come out my mouth and have them represent the best of what I'm – I hear myself – these "words" and I agree it sounds like – I mean, I'm thinking I need to think up a new word, turn a phrase, I don't know, make a, a sound you've never heard before. But I don't have that particular gift. I say it imperfectly and that's why I keep fucking repeating myself, hoping that maybe, somehow, it will come out better, finer and we'll be hearing the same thing, feeling the same —

(**SOPHIE** *has begun to look more frantically for something in particular.*)

SOPHIE. And really the effect you're having, Phillip – is that I feel totally overlooked. You feel incomplete, not me! Where did I put it?!?

PHILLIP. What are you looking for?

SOPHIE. My wallet.

PHILLIP. *(reflexively, wanting to help)* Do you need money?

SOPHIE. No thank you.

(She keeps looking.)

PHILLIP. *(He watches in disbelief – she may really go.)* Sophie. Listen. Listen, it can't just boil down to "let's agree to disagree". We can't just do that.

SOPHIE. And that's why you're keeping me here?

PHILLIP. I'm not keeping you here! I just offered you cab fare for God's Sake.

SOPHIE. You were keeping me here! You were using force to keep me here!

PHILLIP. *(just a fact, not a threat)* Oh, that wasn't force. You wanna see force?

SOPHIE. *(defended)* Go fuck yourself!! Asshole!

PHILLIP. You're getting a little vulgar, Soph.

SOPHIE. That's what happens when you get psychologically and physically abused.

PHILLIP. Oh, C'mon!

SOPHIE. My insurance card. It's in the wallet.

PHILLIP. Look. Look!

(Exasperated at the nearing finality; looking at or holding up one of her paintings.)

It's only a painting!! Is it really that urgent?? I'm not asking why, why is "art" important. I'm not. I'm just asking, Sophie, explain it to me – where is it getting you?

SOPHIE. It's not about where it's *getting me,* just forget it.

(suddenly)

Did you take my wallet? Phillip. Did you? Did you take my wallet??

(He goes to where he's hidden it and gives it to her.)

PHILLIP. I'm not trying to convince you of how meaningful having a child could be –

SOPHIE. Yes, you are.

PHILLIP. No, all I'm asking you to do is to embrace the reality of the child that is here, right here!

SOPHIE. *(simply)* I'm not relating to this as a child.

PHILLIP. That's your problem, not hers. I have answers to your questions. I do.

SOPHIE. I don't have questions.

PHILLIP. You should have.

SOPHIE. I did. I don't have them anymore.

*(She slams the bathroom door. **PHILLIP** stands before the fridge. He begins the daunting task of moving it in front of the apartment door. Re-entering she crosses the room, then noticing:)*

I can't believe you moved the fridge. I can't believe you did that. I need you to move this out of my way!

(He doesn't move)

Fine! I'll do it myself.

*(**SOPHIE** approaches the refrigerator and tries to move it herself.)*

PHILLIP. A baby is a baby whether you relate to it that way or not.

SOPHIE. *(pushing not listening)* ARRRRRRRRGGGGHHHH.

PHILLIP. A baby, which is part mine.

(concerned about her as she pushes)

BE CAREFUL!!

SOPHIE. *(She stops for a second, remove her shoes.)* I'm going to get you arrested! *(repositioning herself)* All right.

PHILLIP. I AM THE FATHER!

SOPHIE. *(gathering strength)* One…

PHILLIP. What would my father have done to keep me? Everything. Anything!

SOPHIE. Two….

PHILLIP. Sophie. We're not talking about a blob of tissue!

SOPHIE. Three! AAAAARRRRRRRRRRGGGGGGG.

(Again, she tries to move it. She's turning red with exertion, overlapping **PHILLIP**'s *next speech.)*

PHILLIP. Whatever is human is human from the beginning. That's a fact!!!

SOPHIE. I'm not as simple as a FACT!!!!!! MOVE, you son of a bitch!

(She stops for a moment, exhausted.)

PHILLIP. I mean, my God, if you really, if you really painted fucking masterpieces, Soph, well then, ok –

SOPHIE. *(This really hurts, everything hurts.)* HELLLLLLLLLLLLP!!

PHILLIP. You argue about the sanctity of making art –

SOPHIE. *(finally surely:)* No, I don't! I'm not arguing the sanctity of anything, I'm only speaking for myself!!

PHILLIP. What's right or wrong can't just be a matter of opinion.

SOPHIE. STOP!!!! Oh God, please make him stop!!!!!!!

(anguished, furiously disappointed, through tears)

I hate that you've done this. *You've* done this!!

(*She's spent. The truth.*)

PHILLIP. (*concerned*) Sophie.

SOPHIE. (*bitter/sad truth*) I hate that you've made me a hater of someone I love.

PHILLIP. Listen, Sophie, how you feel now is not how you may feel one month from now, and by the time the baby is born you may take one look at her and want to give your life to that child.

(*She says nothing. She is exhausted. Sad. Alone. After a long silence.*)

SOPHIE. God, you know what I wish?

PHILLIP. I promise you'll never regret having it. It's not a gamble, Sophie. It's not.

SOPHIE. (*vulnerable, honest, spent*) I wish...I wish I'd never told you. That you never found out. If I'd just kept the whole sloppy thing to myself.

PHILLIP. That would have made me sad. Very sad.

SOPHIE. (*stark*) Well, you couldn't have been sad, if you didn't know about it, could you?!? I would have been sad...alone. And that would have been better. Better than this. I need water.

(*He gets her a glass. She drinks. Sits.*)

Tell me something, ok, tell me honestly, Phillip – in all the years of dating and marriage, you never ever encouraged any other girlfriends or even your wife to have an abortion. Never a mistake? That never happened to you?

PHILLIP. (*beat*) I never did. No. Never.

(*long beat*)

SOPHIE. If I agree –

PHILLIP. What?

SOPHIE. If I agree to, to have it and, let's say you, you take care of it.

PHILLIP. Uh huh.

SOPHIE. I go ahead and have it, and I give it to you –

PHILLIP. I don't understand.

SOPHIE. *(She means this – this is not a trick.)* And you, you raise it, alone.

PHILLIP. *(trying to catch up)* What?

SOPHIE. Because I believe that you want this. At any cost.

PHILLIP. Well.

SOPHIE. What?

PHILLIP. Not at any cost. Sophie, you've just said the word "alone" and it sounds very –

SOPHIE. Final. Yes. But let me ask you. In three months, when I go for the amnio if something is wrong, because the doctor explained that the odds at my age – or it has Downs Syndrome or –

PHILLIP. Is that what you're worried about??

SOPHIE. Phillip, hold on, I'm asking, would you raise a handicapped child?

PHILLIP. *(Things are going too fast for him.)* I'm just trying to catch up here.

SOPHIE. I'm trying to give you what you want –

PHILLIP. This isn't exactly what I want, you know that.

SOPHIE. It's not exactly what I want either, but, what I'm asking, which you haven't answered yet, which is important, because I'll be 43 next month and I'm trying to be thorough about this –

PHILLIP. Alright.

SOPHIE. So, if it were handicapped in some way and I'm not there –

PHILLIP. *(reacting)* Ok, you're not there, all right, I heard you the first time.

SOPHIE. Well, you have to think about that.

PHILLIP. Well, my God, I mean – I'd have to – we'd cross that bridge, wouldn't we?

SOPHIE. We'd cross *what* bridge? I've already crossed the bridge saying I might go ahead. What bridge would you have to cross?

PHILLIP. I'm not going to make choices like that all of a sudden!

SOPHIE. *(affronted)* You want me to make choices, big ones, but you don't have to?!

PHILLIP. Wait. Wait.

SOPHIE. Because, if something were wrong, Phillip, I would not after carrying it for four months – I know myself and I could not abort the pregnancy 16 weeks into it. I would have it and so I'm asking you...

PHILLIP. And I'm saying, all right, yes, for arguments sake, Yes. Yes, I would.

SOPHIE. Not for "argument's" sake, Phillip!! Anything but argument's sake. For the baby's sake, for my sake.

PHILLIP. Oh, *now* it's a baby.

SOPHIE. Would you raise a handicapped child alone or find another woman to help you raise it –

PHILLIP. *(getting angry)* Hold on, hold on a minute, you want me to tell you right now, right this second, would I would raise a disabled, a severely disabled child by myself?? Because, obviously, it's not the best idea in the world –

SOPHIE. *(throwing what he said earlier back in his face, can't resist the nastiness of this)* It's more than an idea. You said so yourself! It's a "developing / human being – "

PHILLIP. You're tossing me curve balls over here.

SOPHIE. Facts, not curve balls. FACTS!

PHILLIP. *(flaring, feeling trapped, the momentum in here will betray them both)* I'd have it. I want it. I WANT THIS CHILD. Not any child. OUR child. Sophie, what are you doing?

SOPHIE. *(disturbed)* I'm listening to you, Phillip. And I hear you say "cross that bridge".

PHILLIP. Because who knows where we'll be four months from now!!

SOPHIE. I hear you say, "Wouldn't be the best idea". Which means what exactly?

PHILLIP. Which means I'm thinking, I'm thinking out loud.

SOPHIE. But, let me ask you, should I go ahead with a pregnancy if, four months from now, you get to decide. Make the "final" decision. All the decisions. For everyone!

PHILLIP. I didn't say that. I never said that!

SOPHIE. *(launched, aggressive)* I mean, it's really upsetting, alarming actually, because, here I've been made to to listen –

PHILLIP. That is not what I said and you know it!!

SOPHIE. *(overlap)* To this holier-than-thou attack on my personal –

PHILLIP. That maybe we'd have come to an understanding by then is what I meant!

SOPHIE. Come to an understanding? We can't come to one now, Phillip. We're going to come to one four months from now?? Come to one ever???

PHILLIP. You want to make this hard. As hard as everything else in your life??? Go ahead!! Be my guest! It could be easy.

SOPHIE. *(the truth)* For you, yes!!! It is easy! *Because you're not the mother, Phillip. You're not the one to get pregnant and carry it, and birth it, and devote yourself to it for the rest of it's life!*

PHILLIP. I'll take care of it. Have it and you're done!

(beat)

SOPHIE. I'm *done?* Wow. Just like that. My God, you just keep dreaming this dream without me, in spite of me, don't you?

(Pointedly – her heart is broken.)

If you can sacrifice me this easily –

(He might move to touch her.)

How could I ever believe you could keep your promise to love anyone?

PHILLIP. *(He's done; he feels tricked, misunderstood. It's war.)* Get out of my way!

SOPHIE. You get out of MINE!!!

(PHILLIP *moves aside and approaches the refrigerator. Tries to move it. As he tries, she talks)*

SOPHIE. *(continuing; bitterly)* Stupid. Rat. Go find another she-thing to have a child with, you hypocrite fake!!

PHILLIP. AHHHHH!

(It won't budge. He's not really trying very hard.)

Lucky for you, you found a little loophole to hang me with, huh? You won. You're the winner.

It'll be easier now, won't it? SO MUCH EASIER! CHRIST! I JUST WANT YOU OUT OF HERE!

SOPHIE. I'll get out as soon as you move the fucking fridge away from the door! C'mon, you moved it over here in the first place!!

PHILLIP. Shit! It's stuck.

SOPHIE. Push it off the other way.

PHILLIP. Well, fucking help me then!

(She starts to help him try to move the fridge as they continue dialogue.)

PHILLIP. *(continuing)* On three!

(They ready themselves on either side of the fridge.)

One. Two. Three.

SOPHIE. Weakling!

PHILLIP. Selfish Bitch!

SOPHIE. Goddamn Liar!!!!

PHILLIP. Cripple!!

SOPHIE. You're the cripple you fucking asshole!!

PHILLIP. ...PUSHHHHHH!!!!!!!

SOPHIE. I ammmmm pushing!!!

PHILLIP AND SOPHIE.

ARRRRHHHHHHHH!!!

(They are both pushing with all their might. Finally, the refrigerator moves slightly. At some point, he takes over, moving it sufficiently away from the door. They are exhausted.)

PHILLIP. Now get out. And take the fucking fridge with you. I don't want it. Go to your appointment! Have a great abortion. Hope it all works out for you. I do. *Get out!!!*

(There is a hush. She puts on her shoes. Her coat. Gets her bag. He is greiving and furious simultaneously.)

And if the only mistake I made was that I wanted to make good on the fucking invitation we made to that little baby – culled from the infinite fucking universe-divine answer to the fucking...

(He cracks.)

I can live with that.

(As she passes him, he grabs her. Shakes her. It is a very violent and threatening motion. We are suddenly aware of his strength. A kind of fury and force even he couldn't have predicted.)

(vehemently, scary, compelled)

I hate you.

SOPHIE. Let go. Phillip. Phillip.

(He releases her. He is spent. She pauses for a moment to steady herself. She collects her bag, and starts for the door.)

I'm...I just need to –

(Her legs begin to give out from under her. She faints. He reflexively catches her in his arms. Nearly an iconic "Prince Charming" catch.)

PHILLIP. Soph. I got you. I got you. You're ok. Sophie.

(The next few moments unfold very slowly. He carries her to the chair. He gets a towel, wets it with water, and cools her head with the towel attentively. When the pain subsides she takes a deep breath, opens her eyes slightly, weakened, but she is clearly going to be alright. After a beat, he kneels beside her. He might take her hand. Or not. They look at one another. Silence – What's just happened to her physically is intentionally ambiguous.)

(Lights fade slowly.)

End of Play